Young Dedalus
General Editor: Timothy

T0014504

Nobody
can stop
Don Carlo

Oliver Scherz

Nobody
can stop
Don Carlo

translated Deirdre McMahon

Young Dedalus

The translation of this work was supported by a grant given by the Goethe-Institut London.

Published in the UK by Dedalus Limited
24-26, St Judith's Lane, Sawtry, Cambs, PE28 5XE
email: info@dedalusbooks.com
www.dedalusbooks.com

ISBN printed book 978 1 912868 02 5
ISBN ebook 978 1 912868 28 5

Dedalus is distributed in the USA & Canada by SCB Distributors
15608 South New Century Drive, Gardena, CA 90248
email: info@scbdistributors.com   web: www.scbdistributors.com

Dedalus is distributed in Australia by Peribo Pty Ltd
58, Beaumont Road, Mount Kuring-gai, N.S.W. 2080
email: info@peribo.com.au

First Published in German as *Keiner Hält Don Carlo Auf* by Oliver Scherz ©
2015 by Thienemann in Thienemann-Esslinger Verlag GmbH, Stuttgart
First published by Dedalus in 2020
Translation copyright © Deidre McMahon 2020

The right of Oliver Scherz to be identified as the author & Deidre McMahon as
the translator of this work has been asserted by them in accordance with the
Copyright, Designs and Patents Act, 1988.

Printed and bound in Great Britain by Clays, Elcograf S.p.A
Typeset by Marie Lane

A C.I.P. listing for this book is available on request.

"How do I get from here to Palermo?" I ask.

The woman at the ticket desk in the station types something into her computer. I shuffle my money-roll from one hand to the other.

"Your next chance would be the 14:29 train to Munich on Platform 3. Then change to the night train to Rome. It arrives there tomorrow morning at 09:25. The connection to Palermo leaves an hour later. Arrival in Palermo Sunday evening twenty-three hundred hours," says the woman at the window.

It only gets to Palermo on Sunday night! How could it take so long? I'd never be back here in time for breakfast on Monday!

"Is there any quicker way?" I ask.

"No, do you want a sleeping car or couchette from Munich to Rome?"

I can't decide. I'm still thinking about Sunday night and twenty-three hundred hours. The woman taps her fingers on the counter.

"Sleeping car or couchette?" she asks again. I've no clue; but it's a bit hard to sleep on the couch at home sometimes.

"Sleeping car," I say.

"That'll be €278.95."

€278?! I've got €210 in my fat money-roll. I emptied out my whole money-box. I thought, half of it would be enough for the train to Palermo! Maximum.

"Would it be a bit cheaper if I don't lie down anywhere and just sit in the passageway?" I ask.

The woman pushes her glasses up onto the top of her head and gives me a funny look.

"How old are you anyhow?" she asks.

"Eleven," I say.

I should have said thirteen! Everybody thinks I look at least thirteen anyway. Especially in my suit, the one I'm wearing now. It's really class, with a white shirt and a tie. I look like an Italian Don in my suit. Don Carlo, the Gangster-Boss and nobody and nothing is going to get in his way. My suit used to belong to Papa. He wore it on special occasions when he was a boy. Now it's mine. And this is my special occasion. I'm going to bring Papa back home.

"Where are your parents?" asks the lady behind

the ticket desk.

"Papa's in Palermo and Mama works in the Old People's Home."

"And your Mama and Papa are okay with you going on such a long journey on your own?"

"I can't tell Mama about it or it would all go wrong." The words just burst out of my mouth.

Whenever I ask Mama when we can visit Papa, she just lists out all his faults and gets as angry as if he were still around. I told her that I was going to stay the night with my classmate Martin and spend all tomorrow with him.

The woman isn't smiling any more. "I'm very sorry, I can't sell you a ticket if your mother or father aren't with you." Then she stops for a moment. "Tell me… did you run away from home, lad?"

I started to sweat. "Nope. I just want to go to my Papa. That's home too."

Why doesn't the woman behind the counter just tell me if I can get to Palermo any cheaper. Somehow everything is going wrong.

"Would you wait a moment, please." The woman goes over to talk to the ticket seller at another desk. They talk quietly, looking over at me. They're very serious. They're against me, that much is clear.

Then the woman comes back. "I'd like to give your mother a call, okay. Can you tell me her phone number?"

I pick up my case and turn around.

Then I run out of the ticket hall, past two security men. They're all against me, for sure. I run even quicker. Straight to Platform 3, up the steps and along the platform, right to the end. At the end of the platform I hide behind the chocolate vending machine; it's the only quiet spot.

Everything is all mixed up in my head. The woman behind the counter, Mama, Sunday night, €278. My plan was much simpler. I just wanted to sit in the train and go. I had the envelope with Papa's address and the picture of his balcony. And I know the map of Italy off by heart. Italy looks like a boot on the map and Sicily looks like a football just in front of its toe. I know exactly where I am going.

For the last five months I've wanted to go to Palermo, for the last five months and six days. Since Papa left because Mama threw him out, in the middle of the night. Now Papa's things are in boxes down in the cellar. At first, I kept bringing them back up.

"No way, Carlo, you can't do that!" Mama said.

"When's Papa coming back?" I asked.

Nobody can stop Don Carlo

Mama just stared at the ceiling looking for an answer. But there are no good answers on the ceiling.

I'm still waiting, always waiting, in school, in bed, at mealtimes. I just can't shake off the words waiting and Papa. But Mama won't go there and Papa won't come here. So, I've got to try it on my own and surprise Papa. But I can't get to him without a train ticket.

"When you want something, Carlo, you have to persevere. Then you can do anything. You just need to really want it. Just do it! And don't think so much!" That's what Papa said to me once on the ten metre diving board. And then he took off – did a cannonball – hitting the water with the biggest splash ever. I've got a photo of him, mid-jump. His gold chain was flying through the air behind him and his sunglasses were perched on his head, like always.

When the Intercity Express comes into the station, I take my case. I can hear Papa's deep laugh as he opens the door in Palermo and finds me there. "You've come here, all the way from Bochum, all on your own! You're something else, Carlo! You're just like me."

I switch off my head, just like I did on that

diving-board. That time I had jumped too, without thinking. Then I see the train like in a haze, as if I were looking through Mama's glasses. Better to look around in a haze rather than see any conductor. Decision made! I'm going without a ticket.

I look down at the ground as I'm getting into the train. Then I walk along the corridor, from one carriage to the next, as far as the restaurant car. As I sit down at a table the train is already pulling out of the station. There's no going back now.

Suddenly our apartment block goes by. I can see my Italian flag fluttering on our balcony. The balcony looks down on the railway. That's where I used to see the Intercity Express trains; it's where I cooked up my plan. Now I'm looking up at the balcony from the train and... tomorrow evening I will be in Palermo. I had really wanted to be back in Bochum by then and have Papa with me. I wanted to take his stuff out of the cellar, all before Mama gets back from her night shift.

A man gives me a funny look, as if he knows that I don't have a ticket. I turn around because I am sweating so much. Right now, I would like to disappear.

There's a dog lying between my feet. He belongs to the woman behind me and has crawled through under the seat. I bend down to him and disappear under the table. The dog is chewing on an old train ticket. He looks up at me lovingly. I like dogs. They don't care whether I have a ticket or not, or that I'm fat. For them the most important thing is getting something to eat. And dogs always think that I have something for them to eat. I pull a slice of pizza out of my pocket. The dog wags his tail and I feel better immediately.

"Tickets please!"

I jump and bang the back of my head on the table. That's a bummer, I feel sick. I never thought the guard would come into the restaurant-car!

I keep my head under the table and look vaguely at the guard's shoes and at the clicker hanging from his belt.

"Help me, doggie," I whisper.

But the dog just swallows the slice of pizza and goes back to chewing the old train ticket. The guard has already finished with the man opposite. "Good day," he calls down to me. "Your ticket please!"

I wriggle out from under the table and stand in front of the guard. My tie is hanging crookedly and the lovely shirt is stuck to my round mozzarella-belly. I've sweated so much that it's nearly see-through around the belly button. If the guard sends me back, the station security men will bring me home to Mama. Then I'll never, ever get to Papa!

"Young man, your ticket!"

"The dog's eaten it," I say suddenly.

Or did I really say that? The guard bends over as if he hadn't understood me properly.

"The dog's eaten it. I can't help it," I repeat pointing under the table.

The guard slowly gets down on his hunkers. And I look down with him. There are only a few soggy bits of ticket on the ground and a couple of scraps hang from the corners of the dog's mouth.

"Impossible…" says the guard.

The woman behind me turns around and pulls the dog back by the lead

"What've you done, Rudi?!" she asks.

"He's eaten the lad's ticket," says the guard starting to laugh.

Now all the other passengers turn around. The woman gives Rudi a slap on the back and pulls a couple of scraps out of his mouth. But nothing can be saved. The whole restaurant car is laughing now, everyone except me and the woman.

"Okay, the dog has already stamped the ticket for me," says the guard and goes on his way, still laughing.

Nobody can stop Don Carlo

But the woman can't calm down. She gives out yards to Rudi and wants me to choose something off the menu. It's her treat. My mouth is dry and my tummy is in knots. I couldn't swallow a thing. All the same I order a thick slice of chocolate cake and a hot chocolate, just so that the woman will leave me in peace.

Eventually everyone stops looking at me, I hang my suit jacket on one of the hooks beside the window to air it. Then I dry out until my belly-button isn't showing through my shirt any more. Outside fields and trees race by. This is like flying, I think. I'm flying from Bochum to Palermo. All I need to do is sit there and let everything fly past me.

I think of Pietro. On my way to the station I went by his pizzeria. Pietro was setting tables out on the path and asked me where I was going. I really hadn't wanted to tell anyone. But Pietro is my second Papa and I'm his fourth son, along with the three real ones, or so he always tells me. Besides he often helps me with homework or we play cards when the pizzeria is closed in the afternoons.

"Palermo!" he shouted, absolutely delighted. "You see! I knew it! Always! Mama's going with you to see your Papa!"

"Nope. I'm going on my own. Mama still doesn't

want to. She doesn't know a thing about it," I said.

Pietro looked my suit up and down. My tie was knotted around my neck like a bootlace because that's the only way I can do it. With a couple of moves he had knotted it properly. Now it hung down like a flattened snake.

"You can't even knot your tie properly but you want to travel alone the length of Europe, and not a word to your Mama?!" he said in Italian-German. "Carlo, you are an absolute rascal! I know how sad you are. And I hope that your Mama and Papa will see sense so that you all get back together again. But really you can't be serious, go on home. Watch a film or play some football. The world is how he is and you cannot change it. I'm twenty years in this restaurant and I must work. I never see the sea even though I want to. The world is how he is!"

"But I can't wait any longer," I said.

"When you finish waiting, what you want just come, all by itself."

"You could come with me. Then you'd see the sea at last," I said.

Pietro laughed even louder than Papa when he heard that.

"I have the sea in a photo behind the bar," he called running to the table. "So, come over here tomorrow. We play a game of cards and talk about everything."

Then, for a joke, he put two slices of pizza into my suit pocket, for the journey home.

Really it would have been much better if Pietro had liked my plan. I really like Pietro but I find it strange that the sea in the photo is enough for him.

The waiter brings the chocolate cake and I get my appetite back, slowly. But when my appetite comes back all's right with the world.

I loosen my tie and try a piece of the cake. It tastes better than all Mama's cakes put together.

I stay in the restaurant car until we get to Munich. Whenever the guard goes by he laughs.

"Your ticket please," he growls at me every time. And when a new guard comes, the waiter tells him the story of the dog and the ticket and he lets me stay sitting there.

The dog-lady has left long ago. She dragged Rudi behind her out of the restaurant car. Rudi slid backwards, to see me longer. Sorry Rudi, I thought. And thank you. Rudi wagged his tail at me and barked goodbye.

Me and dogs, we get on well.

I get off the train in Munich. The station is enormous. There are six InterCity Express trains lined up in a row and there are a lot more snack stalls than in Bochum.

Outside the sun is already going down. I know everyone who works on the little sausage stall in the station in Bochum. I go to a *brezel* stall and buy myself a crisp twisted *brezel* roll. The *brezel*-woman speaks differently from the sausage-woman in Bochum. "Take care m'dear," she says when I'm going, not, "See ya". I think I hear something in English coming over the loudspeakers. I don't understand anything here.

Standing under the noticeboard to eat the *brezel*, I notice there's a train going to Bochum. Pietro would put me on that train straightaway. Because the world is how it is. I think about it; I could get on and go back to Bochum, get into my own bed, go and play cards and eat pizza tomorrow with Pietro.

Nobody can stop Don Carlo

I could hang Papa's balcony photo on the wall like Pietro's sea. I could take down the Italian flag from the balcony, put it away in the cellar with Papa's stuff and stop dreaming about Italy.

"When you stop this always waiting, whatever you wait for just come, all by itself," Pietro said. But I don't believe him. Mama will never come with me to Palermo. Pietro's sea will never come to Bochum. Never, no matter how long he waits. But now I know what I'm going to do. I will dip a bottle into the sea, fill it with sea water and bring it to Pietro as a souvenir.

Suddenly the noticeboard shows the night train to Rome, right down at the bottom. I start to sweat again. 21:03 hours, Platform 12, it says.

I buy myself some pumpkin seeds at a kiosk. I always chew pumpkin seeds when I'm nervous. Then I head towards Platform 12. I sit down on my case on the platform, chewing pumpkin seeds and I look at the photo of Papa's balcony. Papa drew himself with a biro in the middle of his balcony.

"Do you know why we're both so fat?" he asked me the last time he phoned.

"Because of pumpkin seeds," I answered.

"Nonsense. It's so that we can see each other when we wave from our balconies."

Nobody can stop Don Carlo

I thought that was funny. But Papa's balcony is in Italy and mine is in Bochum. Papa often says things that sound good, but don't really mean what the words say.

Mama runs through my head. When she comes to wake me on Monday morning, I'll be sitting beside Papa on the balcony. She'll get an awful fright because I'm not in my bed. She'll phone Martin's mother, and then the police.

Then Papa is in my ear again. "Don't think so much, Carlo. Just do it!"

Papa gets by everywhere. Once he was gone for three days in Bochum. Mama didn't know where he was. That wasn't anything out of the ordinary but what made it so bad was that it was my birthday.

"He even forgets your birthday. He FORGOT YOUR BIRTHDAY!" Mama was even angrier than I was.

"You forgot my birthday," I said to him the next evening when he suddenly turned up again.

"Your birthday?! Carlo!! *Dio mio!* Your birthday!!" he shouted. "Forgot your birthday? Carlo, what do you think? I just postponed it! To today!"

He hugged me tight, fat on fat. He was really strong, just like a bear, squeezing the air out of me. Then he let out a great laugh, that warms my tummy. Papa's laugh can wash everything away and you can't stay angry at him.

"Have you got the tickets for the game?" I asked.

"Tickets for the game! Yes, sure! We just need to pick up the tickets. Let's hit the road straightaway."

"Or is it too late for the game now?"

"It's never too late for anything!" he cried.

Then we rattled off to the stadium on the moped.

The sky was full of floodlights and there was loud cheering and drums beating in the stadium.

At the ticket-desk Papa got really excited. "They won't stump up any tickets for us."

"But you said, we just have to pick them up!" I cried.

"That's true. Now we'll look for Luca. He's our ticket," he said.

Then we walked half-way around the stadium. We found Luca at one of the entrances. He was wearing a neon shirt with "steward" printed on it.

"Luca! Tell us, it's not all sold out, is it? Can you have a look?"

Luca and Papa laughed. Papa knows nearly everyone in Bochum, especially the Italians.

"I can't just let you in. I'd be fired," Luca said.

"Luca! Are you my friend? It's Carlo's birthday

today. It is so important! Do I really have to tell him that we have to go home again?? Carlo wants to be the goalkeeper here, so you'd better be good to him. Now tell me honestly, Luca, are you an Italian or what?"

"Well, I don't know…"

"You don't know? Of course, you're Italian. And when you have a steward's shirt, you have to make use of it."

Papa spent another two minutes persuading Luca, and then, with his help, we were in, over the turnstiles.

We were in before half-time and after the second half there was extra time and penalties. And we won because the goalie saved two penalties. After all that I had no voice left.

"Now we'll collect your present, from the president," Papa said.

He went up the steps with me. Our president sits at the top of the stand, just under the roof of the stadium. A football president is a bit like the king of the club. Papa pushed his way through a row of seats, past important people, until he got as far as the president. Then he spoke to him. I saw it with my own eyes. He pointed at me and talked until the president laughed. Papa and the president were like best buddies!

Another man took us down then, through corridors and down the stadium steps. And suddenly we were in front of the dressing-room. It was just like a dream. The dressing-room's the most sacred place in the world!!! The man pushed me inside to the celebrating players. He caught the goalkeeper and pushed a pen into his hand. And the goalkeeper wrote his name on my keeper's jersey. Right in the middle! With his penalty-saving hands!

"Papa, how did you manage that? How do you know the football president?!" I asked him on the way home, roaring above the noise of the moped.

"Why do you think I know him?"

"Well you were talking to him!"

"Of course, I talk to people. When you want something, you've got to talk to people, even presidents, just like that," Papa bellowed against the wind.

I sit on a bench on the platform and pull my keeper's jersey out of my case. The signature is almost as black as on the first day. I run my finger over it. I can't understand why Papa can't manage to visit me in Bochum, when he could get right to the dressing-room in the stadium. He tells me on the phone that he's coming then nothing happens.

The night train comes into the station! It's dark blue and the brakes screech. I pack my goalkeeper jersey back into the case. The people on the platform surge through the train doors. Suddenly my determination is gone. Whispering through the night into another country, with no ticket or bed is a bit different from eating in the restaurant car. And I remember, from old gangster films, that it's not that easy to get over the border. You need to show passports and open bags, in case of smuggling. And I hadn't even thought of a passport.

The guard whistles, loud and long. The sound goes down into my toes. When the doors beep, I jump up after all and run from the bench to the train. But the doors are closed already by the time I reach them.

"Over here, if you still want to get on," bellows the guard from the last open door.

I look down at the ground while I'm running, so that he won't see my face. It's just too noticeable. Besides me there's no one else running along the platform.

"Next time get in earlier!" grumbles the guard,

as I stumble past him into the train.

I disappear among the people and push my way along the corridor, just to get away from the guard. People grumble at me but I just shove my way onwards. I don't know where to go. There are no seats, only compartments with beds, all made up for other people. At the end of the carriage I disappear into the toilet and splash water from the washbasin onto my face. In the mirror I look like I do after a breaktime fight in the school yard. I'm sweaty and red in the face.

The train shoves me against the wall as it curves its way out of the station. I sit on the toilet seat and look out through a gap in the window. The train wires crisscross the black sky. I'm really on the night train! To Italy! I really can't believe it.

Maybe I can sit on the toilet seat until I get to Rome. And when I change trains I can disappear into a toilet on the next train, right until I get to Palermo.

I straighten up on the toilet seat. I could sleep like that, with my head leaning on the wall. I close my eyes and try to sleep. Only the light is bothering me; there isn't a light switch anywhere.

I pack my suit jacket and sweaty shirt in my suitcase and pull on my keeper's jersey for the night.

Nobody can stop Don Carlo

I leave my tie on to keep Pietro's knot safe. Then I spray a bit of Papa's cologne on my jersey.

I saved the cologne from the bin after Mama's dumping spree. When Mama is on the night shift I sometimes spray some cologne on my duvet. Mama hasn't noticed but she keeps complaining that she can't get Papa's smell out of the flat.

I polish off Pietro's second slice of pizza. My hunger is much bigger than that slice. I could eat up the whole platform snack-machine. First the crisps, then the chocolate bars and jellies.

Suddenly the door opens! The guard! Like lightning I leap to my feet. I feel dizzy like when I'm doing knee-bends in PE, when I can't get enough blood to my head. Did I not lock the door?

There's an old woman standing in the doorway in her nightdress. At least it's not the guard! But nevertheless, I've been discovered!

"Well, I never! But it weren't locked."

The old woman has long white hair, like an Native American. I have to hold tight onto the washbasin so that I don't collapse.

"Are y' poorly lad? Y're as white as a sheet. What's up wi'y?"

"Hunger," I gasp without looking the old lady

in the eye.

"Ah know what that's like. That's yer cir-cu-la-tion. Need t' raise yer legs, y' need sugar. Come on, I got summat for y'."

She comes towards me and just grabs me by the arm and pulls me out of the toilet. I can't do a thing about it; my legs are so weak. Luckily there's no one in the corridor as she pulls me into her compartment.

There's nobody else in the compartment. The woman lays me down on the empty lower bunk and sticks a pillow under my feet. Then she gets a bar of chocolate out of her handbag.

When I finish the chocolate, she gives me a banana and half a slice of marble cake wrapped in a napkin.

"An emergency rescue, that was," says the woman. "Anyway, what's y'name?"

"Carlo."

"Okay, Carlo. Now I'll bring y' back to yer compartment. Which one is it?" The woman talks funny, just like my aunt from Berlin.

"Dunno," I say. I still don't look the woman in the eye, I don't know if I dare. All the same I just want to lie down, I'm so wrecked after the day. I want to lie down and admit everything, just so that I don't have to hide any more.

"Yer compartment number's written on yer booking," says the old woman.

"Haven't got it."

"Give me yer ticket and I'll find it for y."

"Haven't got that either."

"What's that? Who y' travellin' with? Wi' friends or yer parents or what?"

"On my own."

"Stranger and stranger! No booking, no ticket and all on yer own? How's that then?"

I look at the few cake crumbs left on the napkin.

"Did I fish a stowaway outta t' toilet? That it?"

"Think so," I whisper. Now the whole story is out.

"Then we got some talking to do, Carlo. But first I'll give y' t' best tip; get yersel' up on t' top bunk fast and don't even breathe, till t' guard 's gone past. He's about to stick his head in t' door."

The old woman grabs away the pillow from under my feet and shoves me up the ladder. I slide over the bunk to the wall, just as the guard opens the door. As he comes into the compartment and punches the woman's ticket I stop breathing.

"One question," he says then. "Did you see a fat boy anywhere, one with black hair? Someone found a case in the toilet. I think it's his. I noticed the lad getting on the train.

I go cold all over, shivers down my back.

"What's that? What did y' notice?" asks the woman.

"That he's one of these pickpocket types. These guys flit their way through the train and get out at the next stop with their pockets stuffed. There's a suit jacket stuffed with money in the case.

I hardly dare to breathe.

"Y' don't say, now weren't y' t' nosey one! Well I din't see any pickpocket around here," said the woman. "Well what y' goin t' do wi' t' case?"

"Lost property. I'll keep it till Rome. One more thing, you'd better put your handbag under your pillow. Goodnight then."

I hear the guard closing the door and the woman pulls the curtain across the window, "Does t' young man up there need one o' me memory pills?" she whispers up to me. "Forgets t' lock t' toilet door, forgets t' case. Y're a…"

I press even closer to the wall. Case, money, guard, pickpocket… I just don't know what to think.

"Get down here, now!" The woman knocks on my bed. Slowly I push myself out from the wall and climb down the ladder; my legs are shaking like jelly.

"Now, I wanta know what y're really doing here, with yer nicely knotted tie and a case full o' money."

"I'm not a pickpocket!" I say.

"And I'm not a guard. I can see straightaway y're a good lad."

"Is my case gone forever?" I ask.

"No panic. We'll get it back."

The woman is on my side. At least I'm sure of that now.

"Now whisper t' me first what y're doing here."

"I'm on the way to my Papa in Palermo."

"Well, in't that great. And why y' doin' it in secret?"

"Mama doesn't know anything about it. And I'm going to surprise Papa."

The woman's forehead wrinkles up more than ever.

"Yer Mum and Dad know nowt about it?"

"Nope," I say.

And then I tell her that I can't talk to Mama about it, can't talk about Papa or Palermo. And that Papa never comes to Bochum, just sends postcards. And they're scribbled full of writing, with the sentences wriggling around the corners. That's because Papa writes so much about what he wants to do with me, bring me to the casino, eat octopus, go fishing in the sea at night, go on trips on his moped, roast in the sun...

I read the cards over and over again, even though I know them by heart. Then I can hear the waves rolling in and smell the fried octopus and see much more than is written on the cards. I can see me and Papa lying on the beach, like beached whales. There's no one else around. Or we sit on Papa's balcony and slurp spaghetti. Or we chat about how Bochum is no fun without Papa. And how we will trick Mama into coming to Palermo, if nothing else works. I hear Papa's deep laugh. "We'll trick Mama to Palermo, Carlo! That's it! With sun, sand and spaghetti!"

I show the old woman the balcony photo.

"That's where he lives," I say.

"That 'im?" She points at the scribbled biro-Papa, standing waving on the balcony. "Yer Dad's a funny one, eh?"

"Yes, he really is," I say.

"And y're just goin' to 'im, goin' t'all this trouble, jus' for 'im... lad, do y' miss yer Dad so badly?"

"Yes. I really do."

The woman looks out the window, as if she can see something, even though the curtains are closed.

It's ages before she says anything.

"I think that's great, Carlo. What y' dare t' do. I really do. Ah'm 78 years of age and I'm going after the great love of my life. Shoulda done it years ago. Don't even know if he's still alive. But back then, y' see, me in Berlin, 'im in Rome. So far away, it wudn'a do, I thought then. So, we missed each other. Now I think it's my biggest mistake."

The whole time I'm looking at the woman's brown marks. They're everywhere, on her hands and her arms, even on her face. Maybe you get them from waiting too long for someone or missing them all the time.

"Now what are we going to do with you, Carlo? Determination is one thing. But there's other things to think about. Have y' any idea how worried yer Mum is about ye?"

"She thinks I'm staying with a friend," I say.

"And when it all comes out?"

I look down at the cake crumbs again.

"Look here, this is what we'll do: we'll let yer Mum sleep on for a while and ring her early tomorrow morning. I'll help y'. She has t' know, ye know." The woman catches my chin and lifts my head so that I'm looking at her face and not at the crumbs. "D'y' agree?" I nod.

"Good. An' now let's get yer' case back. The guard can have his pickpocket, if that's what he wants.

A minute later I'm standing behind our sliding door, waiting. The old lady is already at the end of the corridor. I'm so excited I nearly pee my pants. She calls the guard until he comes out of his compartment. Then she tells him that the tap in the toilet is broken. That's her plan.

"There in't a drop of water coming outta' t' tap!"

"Did you press the button?" asks the guard.

"What button? There's no buttons on t' tap. Come and see."

The guard shakes his head and goes into the toilet with the woman, just like she said he would.

Now it's *my* turn! I whizz down the corridor, like a gangster in a chase, straight into the guard's compartment. Quick as lightning I look around, behind the chair, under the table, left, right. Where's that case? My heart thumps in my ears. I open the cupboard. And there it is! My case!

I grab it out of the cupboard and slam the door shut again. Then I whizz back down the corridor, without turning around.

Back up on my bed and under the cover. My

heart is still thumping, right until the old woman comes back.

"Well, it's a good thing, that I look t' way I do, as if I han't a clue about how t' world works," she says, knocking on my case. "Y' got it. Well done. Y'd get by as a pickpocket." She giggles like a girl, not a bit like an old woman.

"Thanks!" I whisper.

"No problem. An' now let's get some sleep. We've got important stuff to sort out in t' morning…"

I don't know how I could close my eyes now.

I still can't sleep even though the old woman has been snoring for ages.

My phone beeps. It shows: *Welcome to Austria*. I'm in a different country! Without a passport and with a case that's been searched. I hold my case tight and look at the holes in its lid. I'm tired out. But I can't stop thinking about Papa and Mama and how he was thrown out, in the middle of the night. I often think about that before falling asleep. Mama just chased Papa out of the flat, down the stairs and out the door. Even though she's really a little fly and Papa's a bear.

I shut myself into my room for three days afterwards. "Carlo, talk to me, please. It's not all my fault," Mama called through the door.

I often used to ask myself how a bear could let himself be chased off by a fly. A bear would only do that, if he felt pretty small himself, if he had a really bad conscience. Maybe Papa wasn't really hunted away, maybe he just skived off. I don't know anything about love but I know there are lots of rules about it. Mama knows them all. She used to explain them all to Papa, up and down, through and through, in German-Italian and Italian-German. But Papa never kept the rules, that's certain. And maybe he just skived off from love. Maybe.

During the night I dream that I phone Mama. I'm sitting on the moped behind Papa and shouting into the phone, that everything is going well.

"Carlo, you haven't a clue, you've no idea how worried I am," shouts Mama back. "Come home immediately!!!"

But Papa and I race through Palermo, through every red light, away from the police chasing us, we're heading straight for a cliff.

"*Arrivederci!*" roars Papa, waving at the police.

Then we're right over the cliff on the moped. The cliff is more than a hundred meters high. The moped flies off beneath us along with Mama on my phone. Papa and I fall for a whole minute, our legs stretched out. Then we do the biggest cannonball ever, down into the sea.

When I wake up Mama is still in my head. It's bright outside already, but the old lady's still snoring on. I twist and turn, towards the wall and back again. "We'll ring her early tomorrow morning," the woman had said. Maybe Mama won't be raging if I ring her. Maybe she'll start to cry, because I just left, without a word, like Papa always did, or because she's worried that something happened to me. And what if she bawls her eyes out, like she did when she threw Papa out? I used to think she would never be happy again.

I take my case and slither towards the ladder, moving as quietly as I can so that I don't wake the old woman. Then I climb down the ladder and slip on my trainers.

The brown spots on the old lady's face are still there. I can't wait around for Papa until I get brown spots.

"I'm really sorry, but I just have to go," I whisper. I would much prefer to say a proper goodbye to the woman. "But this is the only way."

Nobody can stop Don Carlo

I run through all the carriages, right to the end
of the train, as far away from the guard and the
woman as possible. I really like the woman but I'll
only phone Mama when I'm safely in Palermo. I'll
ring from Papa's balcony, with Papa's help, before
Mama discovers my empty bed.

I'm the very last one off the train in Rome, right at the end. Most of the passengers run towards the main concourse. I get behind a pillar. Luckily, I don't see the guard. I look at the old woman's back until she disappears in the crowd.

Then I put on my sunglasses and throw my suit jacket over my shoulder. Don Carlo is in Italy. I come from here, I can feel that straightaway, even though I was never here before. Italy is in me, from Papa. He's a real Sicilian. And so am I, at least, half of me is.

I stroll onwards. Everything around me is Italian, the sun, the people, the advertisements and the announcements on the loudspeakers. I understand them, I'm half-Italian and I half-understand Italian:

"…there's a connection for the Intercity Express to Palermo at 10:33, Platform 2…"

I look at the station clock. It's 10:30! I get the

shock of my life. My phone also says 10:30! The woman in the ticket office in Bochum told me I had an hour before my train for Palermo left! How come it's only three minutes?

A notice beside the clock says, *"Rittardo"*. Delayed! The night train was late. Everything's late in Italy, Mama says. How can I get from Platform 28 to Platform 2 in three minutes?!!

I run, just like all the other passengers had, the whole length of the platform, back the whole length I had earlier run through the train, and even further until I got to the first carriage. At last I get onto the concourse and I run on, past all the platforms. 27... 26... 25... there are a lot more platforms in Rome than in Bochum! And there are many more people that I need to dodge around.

The clock again. Two minutes more. 19... 18... 17... by Platform 12 I can't run any more, I've got such a stitch in my side.

When I can breathe again I have only half a minute left. At Platform 8 I can see my train. I force my legs on, 7, 6, 5, 4, 3... and turn onto Platform 2. I get as far as the door of the train and press the button. But the door won't open.

"I have to get on! I! Just! Have! To!" I wheeze and press the button again. Then the train leaves without me.

The rear lights of the train swim in front of my eyes. I'm so furious, at the night train and at my slow legs.

What can I do now? I walk up and down the platform, past the boards with the train times and destinations. I read all the timetables through but I can't find any other train to Palermo.

There's no Palermo either on the announcement board in the hall.

I walk out onto the square in front of the station.

Buses blast past, throngs of cars and mopeds weave in and out. Everything here is too fast.

Maybe there's a bus that goes to Palermo. But the bus-drivers shake their heads or tell me that I need to take the train.

Furious, I shunt pigeons out of my way and see a plane in the sky. A plane wouldn't work either. Nothing works.

"Taxi?" somebody asks me suddenly. A man comes towards me. "Bochum... great!" He points at my keeper's jersey with the Bochum crest on the back. "Taxi, taxi?"

I had never even thought of a taxi, but maybe Palermo is too far.

"I'm going to Palermo," I say.

"Hotel Palermo, no problem."

"No! To Palermo. Sicily. On the football."

"Palermo, Sicily?!" The taxi driver gives me a funny look.

Quickly I take out my money-roll. I've no idea how dear a taxi is. But I'd spend everything just to get there. I leaf through the roll, pausing at the fifty euro note, so that he can see it properly. I pull the *brezel*-change out of my pocket too.

"Is that enough?"

My money-roll makes a real impression. The taxi driver thinks for a minute and chews his gum even faster. Then he nods. He nods!

"Good, okay," he says. "No problem. Palermo, Sicily. Come on."

He takes my case from me and runs towards the taxi. Right away I'm ten kilos lighter. Maybe this will work. Palermo here I come!

"Is the taxi as quick as the train?" I ask as I run after him.

"Taxi, fast, *si, si*, my taxi faster than train."

My case lands in the boot of the taxi. The boot only closes at the third slam because there are two big dents in the back of the car.

Then I'm sitting back in the taxi.

Nobody can stop Don Carlo

As we career across Rome, I really believe in Palermo again. The taxi horn honks all the cars out of the way and goes through traffic lights, even when they've already turned red. I hold on tight to the grip above the window and keep looking straight ahead so that I don't feel sick.

Then we're out of Rome. Suddenly all around me looks like Papa's postcards. There are hills and olive groves everywhere. Warm air streams in through the window; it smells like the herbs for spaghetti-bolognese. I stretch my head out the window and let my mouth fill with air. This is the land of Papa, Pietro and pizza. People here love food, just like me. You can even ride a moped on your own when you're eleven, Papa says, and when you've got a problem, you only need to ask your neighbours.

"Will we get to Palermo in time for supper?" I ask the taxi driver in Italian. In the wing mirror I look like a real Italian, with my black hair and sunglasses. The only thing missing is Papa's gold chain.

"*Si, Si*," says the taxi driver looking back at me.

I sink down further into the soft seat and let my arm hang out the window. It's better in the taxi than on the train, with the window open and the music on the radio. My tie flutters in the wind, the fields race by. Nothing else is going to stop Don Carlo. I shoot with my fingers into the wind. Bang-bang!

We're driving along when the taxi suddenly judders to a stop.

"*Merda!*" The driver punches the steering wheel. "Car broke down, always broke down..." He turns the key in the ignition but the engine doesn't start. "No good... gotta push... behind... I'll do the accelerator," he says to me.

"Okay," I say. I don't want to lose a second.

The taxi driver takes my suit jacket so that it won't get dirty. Then I get out and brace myself behind the car.

"*Uno, due, tre!*" the taxi driver calls out the window.

I push so hard that the stones under my trainers bounce away down the lane. The engine starts straightaway and the taxi takes off! I raise my arms high as if I'd scored a winning goal, until the taxi driver disappears around the next bend.

I wait. The taxi driver must be doing a loop to get the engine running properly again. I brush the dust off the bottoms of my suit trousers.

Another minute goes by and the taxi still doesn't come back. Maybe it just stopped again. I go around the corner. There's no taxi there. It's not around the next corner either.

I get hot all over. What if the taxi driver doesn't come back because Palermo has suddenly got too far for him. But then he just wouldn't disappear like that. He'd want the fare from Rome to here, at least, … my money-roll! Where is it anyway? It isn't in my trousers pocket. THE SUIT JACKET! IN THE TAXI! MY SUIT JACKET AND MONEY-ROLL ARE STILL IN THE TAXI! AND SO IS MY CASE!!! I feel dizzy. I almost collapse. I pull my tie over my head and hurl it into the dust on the ground. HAS HE STOLEN THE LOT?

I hardly ever cry. But now I can't help howling.

I'm usually good at recognising mean tricks, being laughed at, sideways looks, stupid sayings and so forth. I'm used to that because I'm fat. But this is something else. It's much, much worse. He tricked me out of the taxi, got me to help even though there was nothing wrong with the engine! And then I really bawl my eyes out.

I turn around in a circle. There are olive trees and hills all around. Far away, between the hills I see the spire of a church tower. There's nothing else around. I fix my eyes firmly on the church steeple but everything in my head keeps spinning on. "Whenever you have a problem, you just need to ask the neighbours," Papa would say. But there aren't any neighbours here. Nobody helps anyone else in Italy!

I need to breathe a bit more slowly or everything spins faster. Somehow, I try to think like Papa. Right now, he would phone someone in Rome; he'd know someone to ring.

I pull out my phone. Luckily it was in my trouser pocket. The numbers in my phone are my aunt in Berlin and Martin. They're no good to me now; neither is Mama. There's only one other person I know, that I'd like to call now. I just need to speak to someone right now.

I blow my nose and press the number.

"Ristorante da Pietro!" calls Pietro down the phone. His voice sounds just like at home. "Hallo? This is *Ristorante da Pietro*. Who's there?"

"I…"

"Carlo? That you?"

"Yes…"

"You gotta speak up. I can hardly hear you. You sound like you're in Italy!" Pietro laughs at his joke. "Carlo, I have a full restaurant here, you have to be quick to tell me what you want."

The crickets are chirping all around me. I don't know where I am, just that I'm somewhere in Italy.

I can't tell Pietro that…"

"I… I don't think I can make it to play cards today…" My throat is too tight for talk. There's nothing I want more than to sit with Pietro at a table in his pizzeria, to play cards and to tell him about the train guards and the taxi driver. Or tell him that I'm up to my neck in trouble and I can't get out of it on my own, just like he said. I can tell Pietro about the worst things. But it's different on the phone.

"Carlo," says Pietro, "you sound like you lost a football match. What's wrong?"

I take a deep breath.

"All my money's been stolen!" I say.

"Your money! Stolen!"

"It was in my jacket pocket. Now it's all gone!"

My nose is running again.

"You have to calm down, Carlo. Take it easy. You'll find your money, for sure. It's probably in another jacket, or under the sofa."

"I can't get to Palermo without my money…"

"You shouldn't go to Palermo without your Mama, I told you already. Now listen up: you come around to me this afternoon. Then we talk everything over. I don't have time right now. But food is never so hot in your mouth as when it just cooked. It'll all work out."

Nobody can stop Don Carlo

I hear Italian music from the pizzeria, same as every other day.

"But I… I don't know if I can make it over to you later. I'm… because… I'm…" I can't say it on the phone. Talking doesn't solve anything; I need to see Pietro's face. Otherwise he'll get the wrong end of the stick because I haven't done as he told me."

"You've lost it a bit at the moment. Calm down now. You come over to me in a while. I keep a slice of lasagne hot for you and then the world seem a better place. And if your money don't turn up, I'll dip into my till, *capito*? Now I got to look after my customers, okay?"

"Yeah… yeah…"

"I tell you, it will all work out. *Ciao*, Carlo! See ya later! Keep your head up!" Pietro hangs up.

His voice is gone and my nose is full again. I pick the tie up off the ground. The knot is still right because Pietro always does things properly. I should have listened to him yesterday. "Go on home instead. Watch a film or play some football. The world is how he is."

And what if I never make it back to Bochum? What if I never get out of here?

I set off in the direction of the church tower. At least I still have the *brezel*-change in my trousers pocket, seventeen euros and forty cents. Maybe there's a bus back to Rome from the church tower, or maybe not.

I still have my phone in my hand. And now I have my thumb over *Mama*. But what if she cries or shouts at me. Mama is the last resort. She's always there when there's nothing else left. Whenever I'm sick or something goes wrong in school, she sorts it out. She would just get into her car and come and get me.

I stand there and wipe my eyes. There's nothing in front of me, not even a house, not a soul.

I just can't go on. I can't get to Palermo. My money-roll, the address and the photo of Papa's house are all gone. I wouldn't even find the balcony!

Suddenly I can't even wait to get as far as the church tower. I want to tell Mama that I need her more than ever, and press the button. The phone dials Mama's number… and then… I see MY CASE!! It's in the bushes at the side of the path. It's open, my white shirt and the cologne lying beside it on the ground. I press the red button before the phone rings and run towards the bushes. Papa's cologne bottle is still in one piece! I spray some on my tummy. It's still working.

My suit jacket is in the bushes too!! I fish it out

and right away run my hands through the pockets. But the money-roll isn't there. The taxi driver really did steal it! And the jacket is a bit the worse for wear; there's a rip in the sleeve.

I take the balcony photo and the envelope out of the pocket. The envelope is crumpled but you can still read the address:

Via Sant'Agostino No 9 – 90100 Palermo

I pull on my jacket. I don't care about the heat any more. I hang my dusty tie around my neck. Now I look a bit like Don Carlo again. I fold my white shirt and put it back in the case.

Suddenly I hear a tractor. I'm not completely alone here then. As the tractor comes around the bend, I get out of its way. But it doesn't go past. Instead it stops beside me in a thick cloud of dust. There's a boy sitting at the steering wheel. He's not much older than me.

"*Ciao!* Everything okay? I can give you a lift into the village, if you want," he says in Italian and laughs.

I sit on the tractor above the big wheel, beside Matteo. Matteo really is only fourteen. Even so, he's such a cool driver; it looks like curving the tractor around corners is just everyday stuff for him.

We turn off the lane onto a bumpy field and the tractor shakes the stuffing out of me. The church tower bounces in front of me, all over the place, just like my thoughts. I'm going from Mama to Papa to Pietro and from Bochum to Palermo and back.

I tell Matteo about the taxi driver, how he robbed me and how I'll never get to Palermo now. Matteo gets really mad about the taxi driver. He even thinks that he beat me up when he sees the tear in my sleeve. I like Matteo straightaway. He looks like a thin version of myself. He's got short black hair too and a wide mouth for laughing.

"My family will help you out," he says. "No worries! I'll take you home with me."

I don't tell Matteo that I need to phone Mama

because there's no one else to help me. I let my thoughts go on swirling around.

At the farmhouse we spring down from the tractor.

"I hope you're hungry," says Matteo running ahead of me into the farmhouse. It looks old. Inside there's a wooden wheel hanging on the wall in the hallway, beside a black and white Grandpa in a thick wooden frame.

Matteo leads me into a room with a long table laden down with food and with people around it.

"My family," says Matteo.

I can't believe that this is a single family; there are so many people around the table. And behind the table, in the corner, there's a Grandma in an armchair.

Matteo's mother is the first to notice me. At least I think that it's his mother. She asks me my name, and Matteo tells her how I've been robbed and beaten. Suddenly it all goes quiet around the table and everyone listens as he tells them about the taxi driver's trick.

"*Bambino, bambino!*" says the mother after the story. She wipes the dirt off my suit jacket and strokes my face, just like my own mother would.

Then she sits me down at the table, pushing a

plate in front of me. It's full of steaming pasta with ham sauce, and there's tomato salad and white bread to go with it.

I can't touch a thing. There are looks coming from everywhere. When the three girls at the table start asking questions, I look down at my plate. I tell them that I come from Germany and that I want to go to Palermo to my Papa. I say I'm fourteen like Matteo. It sounds a bit better to be travelling on your own when you're fourteen.

"Why are you wearing a tie over your tee-shirt and trainers with a suit?" the girls ask.

Luckily their mother stops them: "Let the boy eat in peace."

The steam from the sauce goes up my nose while Matteo's brothers complain about the taxi-mafia and the police. There's no point in ringing the police, they say, the police won't do anything about it.

"Why did you want to go by taxi anyway?" asks one of the brothers.

"Because the train from Rome was gone already," I say.

Then they all start talking at the same time. I'm not good at fast Italian. I only understand that a taxi is far too dear and that there is a train from Rome to

Naples every hour.

"The ferries only go in the evening. You would easily have caught the ferry with the next train," says one of the brothers.

What's this about ferries and Naples? I can't understand a thing!

"I didn't know there was a train every hour," is all I say.

"Or was your ferry ticket stolen too?"

I shake my head. I have no idea what to admit. If I say that I don't even have a ticket, they'll only ask even more questions. They'll all have questions from the smallest girl to the biggest brother and if they realise that I'm on the journey without telling anyone, then that really would be a case for the police.

I take a big gulp of my juice. I nearly have to spit it out again. It's wine! Does everyone here drink wine, even Matteo and the girls?

"Let's just take him to *Napoli*!" suggests Matteo. And the father looks at the oldest brother.

"Why not," he says.

I think about my map of Italy. From Naples to Palermo across the sea is much shorter than taking a train right down the length of the boot. I never even thought of a ferry! I feel in my pocket for my *brezel*-change. Would it be enough to get across the sea on the ferry?"

I can feel the wine going into my legs, even though I only had a mouthful.

"First you tell your parents what's happened to you." says the Mama, handing me a phone. But I'm still only thinking about the ferry.

"I… can't ring," I say, "…Mama's asleep till the afternoon because she's on the night shift. She turns the phone off." That bit is true, at least.

"And your Papa?"

"I can't get through. I did try. I point to my phone and look down at my plate again."

"No problem," says the father, because one of the boys will get me to the ferry on time and I'll arrive in Palermo alright. "We'll bring you to *Napoli*." And he lifts his glass in the air.

"Saluté!" everyone shouts suddenly and drinks a toast to me. Me too!

And then the family all introduce themselves by name, Mama Giulia and Papa Edoardo, three sisters and four brothers; there is an Uncle Michele too. The brothers have carried the grandma in the armchair to the table; she's called Francesca. The only one missing is Grandpa Giuseppe from the picture in the hall.

Nobody can stop Don Carlo

I look across at the Papa. He's dunking his bread straight into the sauce dish. His hands show signs of all his work in the fields, with clay in the cracks of his skin. His face is brown and has wrinkles that laugh even when he's not laughing.

"You still have to go across to Philippe on the tractor," he shouts across to Matteo. It's great to have a Papa at the table, it really is.

I'm going to have such a big family when I grow up, with all this laughing and chatter in the house, just like here. It will never be as quiet in my house as it is at home.

I'm going to have at least three children. They can be as noisy as they like. And I'll dunk my bread in the sauce and tell them stories, about Palermo, gangsters and all about how I brought Papa back to Bochum.

I'm getting warm from all the hot pasta and the wine. The wine really tastes good because it's sweet. And it's making my head fuzzy; I feel like talking more than ever.

When my mouth isn't full I tell them about Pietro, who makes the best pizza in Germany because the dough is Italian. It's thin and crispy, not thick and soggy like everywhere else in Bochum. I'm going to be a restaurant chef, just like Pietro, I tell them, preferably in Italy, because I love food.

The Mama ladles another helping of pasta and ham sauce onto my plate. She's delighted I'm enjoying it so much.

And suddenly I start talking about Papa, that he's the best salesman in the world. He can sell anything, I say, car tyres, mattresses, bicycles, computers, fish and vegetables. When Papa is dealing, he can always get the best price. He got olive oil so cheaply that the whole cellar was full of it; there was even some in my bedroom. It was there for a whole year! In the end, he even had to give oil to his friends as presents. And he always has the cellar full of stuff he gets from his friends. Even the Football-President is his friend.

I tell the story about the Football-President on my birthday, the way Papa tells stories, waving my hands and with proper expression on my face. Then I show them the signature on my keeper's jersey. Even the girls think this is great and Grandma Francesca laughs so much that you can see her only tooth.

Matteo's family is cool. Papa would like them too. You can make noise when you're eating here, dunk your bread in the sauce, drink wine and drive tractors. And Grandma Francesca is there, right in the middle of it all.

I'd love to stay longer with Matteo's family. But I can't, because of the ferry. Then I think of dessert; I definitely want some of that.

I'm the first one to finish my ice cream.

"Can we leave straight after the meal?" I ask.

When we're back in the yard, standing by the car, my case feels three times as heavy as before. It's full of water, bread, a big chunk of ham and a bottle of olive oil for Papa.

The Mama gives me big sloppy kisses on the left and right cheeks, then I get into the car with big brother Bernardo. The whole family waves me off, even Grandma Francesca. I lean out the window and look back, so that I can see them all, until we turn the corner.

On the journey Bernardo explains how you get the best oil out of the olives. I think that's important, for when I'm a chef.

But I can't keep my eyes open, they just close.

I dream that Mama is sitting on Papa's shoulders. Papa is dancing with her, all around our flat. The music is so loud, that you could hear it all the way down to the street. And Mama bends to one side, so

that she doesn't bump into the light on the ceiling.
I hold my arms out in case she falls because she's
laughing so much. But she doesn't fall even though
we are spinning so much that, at last, we all fall
onto the bed, dizzy. I'm lying on the bed in between
them. On my left, I can feel Papa laughing, on my
right Mama's laughing too. There's nothing better
than lying between them. I spread myself out so
that I can feel more of their laughing in my tummy.
I lie like that for hours.

I wake up. I've no idea how long I've been asleep
for. My phone rings. It rings and rings. I pull it out
of my pocket. MAMA!! I nearly drop the phone.
Mama knows that I'm not at Martin's is the first
thing that comes into my head. Maybe she met his
mother in town, or maybe Martin called to ask me
to play football.

"Something important?" asks Bernardo.

I shake my head and look out the window until
the ringing stops. Why's Mama ringing me now,
when there's a ferry and she didn't ring earlier.

I get a text. I don't dare to open it. Later, when
we are racing along the motorway, I open it.

"How did last night go?" it says. *"I had a bad night.
Are you gone to football? You forgot your football boots.*

Nobody can stop Don Carlo

Do you want me to bring them to you? There's food in the fridge in case we don't see each other later. I need to leave again at six. XX Mama."

I sink down into the seat, really deep. Mama didn't notice a thing! I roll the window down and shovel warm air into my face. Maybe Mama's standing in front of the shoe rack, in her nightdress because she's on night shift. I want to give her a hug, right now.

I'd really like to text back and say that I'm not at Martin's but am sorting something out for us, that it's going to be the way it was in my dream, with Mama on Papa's shoulders, with music playing and lots of laughter. That's what I'm bringing back for us!

"Hi Mama. Night was good. Martin's lending me boots. Staying with him tonight too. Thanks for the food. See you tomorrow. Hope shift goes well. C."

I can't write any more, not yet.

"There's the sea." Bernardo points out the window.

I see glimpses of blue between the houses. We're in Naples already and are heading down to the docks, following the signs for the ferries.

Then suddenly it's there in front of us: Pietro's sea! I've never seen the sea before. It goes as far as the sky and doesn't stop at the sides! You wouldn't know that from the photo in Pietro's pizzeria. The photo should cover the whole wall! I'm going to tell Pietro that. It should go from the bar all the way to the window!

Bernardo stops in front of the departures hall for the ferries.

"I'll bring you as far as the right exit, okay? Where does your ferry leave from? Show me your ticket?"

"No, it's okay. I can manage," I say quickly and grab my case.

Bernardo doesn't really know what to do. But I make him see that I know my way around travelling on my own. "Thanks a million for bringing me. When I open my restaurant, I'm going to invite you all, the whole family, with Grandma Francesca and everyone else. I promise."

Bernardo laughs at that, but I'm deadly serious.

"Well then," he says and shakes hands. "Have lots of fun with your Papa."

I slam the car door and head for the hall. Bernardo only drives off when I turn around and wave.

When you're only eleven you've no chance of doing things. Clearly, I wasn't getting anywhere with the woman behind the ticket desk. Women at ticket desks never give me tickets, whether they're in a stadium or a station. And this one just told me I couldn't even travel on the ferry on my own until I was eighteen.

Now I'm standing outside at the wire fence. The ferries are in the port, on the other side of the fence. They are bigger than our apartment block in Bochum and there's black smoke pouring out of their chimneys.

The ferry in front of me has PALERMO written in big thick letters on its side. It's tied up at the end like a huge garage. An aeroplane could fit into it! And I need to get in there; I've just got to!!

A man, dressed in white, from head to toe, is standing just in front of the ferry. He's whistling signals as trucks reverse into the ferry. Everyone, except the wild dogs, obeys his referee's whistle. The dogs prowl between the trucks just as they like.

Fifty metres to my left there's a gate with men in uniform standing in front of it. If I were a dog I could scuttle in past them and past the man in white too. I could just walk on to the ferry.

One of the dogs comes up to the fence and stands in front of me. I'm sure he's smelt the ham in my case.

He bends his head low and gives me a loving squint, just like Rudi in the train yesterday.

"Is there any way you can help me out?" I ask him, taking ham out of my case.

The dog wags his battered tail. But the chunk of ham won't go through the fence. The dog slinks along the fence and suddenly appears over on my side of it. At first, I can't imagine how.

"How... how did you get through the fence...?" I ask as the dog disappears off with the ham.

I find the hole right away. A piece of the fence has rusted through, right at the bottom. I crouch down in front of the hole. A dog can get through, and a case. But what about a mozzarella-belly?

The man in white is still busy with the trucks and the men in uniform are chatting over at the gate. No one notices me pushing my case through.

Nobody can stop Don Carlo

I don't find doing forbidden stuff so hard any more. I only need to think of Papa laughing when he opens the door to me. And I can't help it if I need a ticket to get to him. Nobody else in my class needs a ticket for his Papa, only me.

I slither on my belly across the ground, over to the other side. The wire rips the back of my suit jacket. But I'm through, just the same. On the other side of the fence I button the jacket over my tummy so that I don't look a complete scruff-bag. I stuff my tie under my jersey. I keep the man in white in my sight. He whistles to signal a huge truck across the square. A proper gangster would hide by hanging under the truck. But I always fall off straightaway whenever we're supposed to be climbing ropes in PE. I need to run, to get into the ferry somehow, without being noticed. I look at the ground as though I had lost something. That gains me a couple of metres.

Suddenly there is a bang. It sounds just like a shot. I freeze to the spot. For a second I think the guys in uniform are shooting at me. I hear people screaming. And then I see two men roaring at each other. The man in white whistles and bellows at the pair of them. The two trucks behind them have bumped into each other. The bigger truck has crashed into a smaller one and half its load has slid off. There are wooden pallets and boxes of fruit everywhere. Apples and oranges are rolling all over the place; the place is full of them! Some even roll almost as far as me.

People come running. Somebody gathers up oranges. There's just another couple of metres to go. He looks at me as if I were stupid, just standing there. So, I start to help him. I collect so many oranges that I have a mountain of them in my arms by the time I get as far as the trucks. There's complete uproar. The driver is still shouting. The man in white is shouting into his walkie-talkie and someone comes out of the ferry pushing a trolley. I pack my oranges into the orange box, just like the other people. We load the boxes of oranges onto the trolley, until it's full. By that time sweat is rolling down my face. Then I stand there, nothing in my hands and don't know what to do next.

"Grab onto the front, otherwise the whole thing will topple over again!" says the guy pushing the trolley. Off he goes and I realise, he means me.

I run to the front of the trolley, grab hold of it and stumble backwards. I can't slip up now! Can't let any boxes fall or trip up while I'm running backwards. I just need to keep going, as far as the ramp, and in through the huge snout. If that works, I'm there! I'm on the ferry!!

"Now we have to pull all this garbage in on foot. Rats!!" says the guy as we rattle up the ramp onto the ferry.

"Rats!!" I say at the same time.

My case is still out there, right where I picked up the first oranges! I can't go back though! If I go back, then I'll never get up the ramp again!!

I can't let the case out of my sight, Papa's cologne, my white shirt, all the stuff from Matteo's family! It's all gone! I'm just lucky that I'm wearing my keeper's jersey.

The case gets smaller and smaller as we burrow our way into the ferry. Then it disappears between people and trucks.

"Are you one of Rizzoli's people?" the trolley guy asks me while we're waiting for the lift.

I nod and hope that he doesn't ask me anything else.

"Which league?" He points at my Bochum jersey.

"Bundesliga," I say casually.

I don't think that this guy is that old, about seventeen or so. Suddenly his eyes open wide.

Nobody can stop Don Carlo

"German *Bundesliga*?! Germany's got the best teams in the world!" He says. "Is that a good team?"

"The best in the whole of Germany," I say.

When we're standing in the lift with the trolley, Adriano tells me all about his team from Palermo. He pushes up the sleeve of his cook's jacket to show me a tattoo on his arm and I show him the keeper's signature on my jersey.

"That's from the Number 1 in Germany," I say, because that's what he is, for me.

Adriano gives me the thumbs up. If you chat about football, you have friends everywhere, Papa always says.

When I tell him that I have a season ticket for the stadium and go to all Bochum's home games, Adriano gives me a funny look. He looks at Pietro's tie knot sticking out from under my jersey, at my suit-trousers and the torn jacket.

"Every home game in Bochum..." he repeats. "And you're one of Rizzoli's people, yeah right? And you're not even from Naples, are you? You're from Germany, aren't you?"

"I... I'm half-Italian..."

"You're too young to be working!"

"I'm fifteen..."

"Yeah right! What on earth are you doing here?"

Now I'm really in a panic. Adriano doesn't sound nice any more. And if I'm not his football friend, just a liar standing there, he'll bring me to the man in white.

Adriano's waiting. I need to say something. He's not going to believe me any more if I say I'm one of Rizzoli's people. I can only tell the truth; I can't think of anything else. I look Adriano straight in the face. And then I tell him as much about Mama and Papa and my plan as I can while we're in the lift. And I tell him the rest as we roll the trolley into a room full of food and unload it. I help Adriano like a world champion, because of our football friendship.

"Can't you hide me someplace? Please!" I ask after the last box is unloaded.

"Why should I believe your story about your Papa?" asks Adriano.

"It's true. I swear on my jersey!"

Adriano thinks about this, his eyes narrow to slits. "Okay. Then I want your jersey."

"My keeper's jersey??!!"

"If it's not worth that much to you, then your story isn't true," says Adriano. "You can hide yourself behind the boxes, in exchange for the jersey."

I try to get my head around this. My jersey is

worth more than anything to me!

"Can't I give you something else?" I pull the seventeen euros out of my pocket, but Adriano shakes his head.

"It's much too risky for me to hide you here. I'll only do it for the signature," he says.

My belly goes into knots. The jersey or Palermo. I've no choice. I smell Papa's cologne as I pull the jersey slowly over my head, just like our keeper does when we lose a match.

"Here…" I whisper. My voice is gone. I give the signature a last kiss. Then I'm standing there in my vest.

I've got to sit on the ground behind the boxes of fruit, so that no one will see me. Don't you dare come out and don't touch any of the food, Adriano said. And he'll collect me at the end of his shift, at midnight. By then there won't be anyone left in the kitchen and we can go through it. He comes in a couple more times with more loads of fruit. Then he turns out the light and closes the heavy door behind him. I hope he doesn't forget all about me.

I've hardly any space behind the boxes. And there's nothing to do. I think about my jersey, and the case. Then back to the jersey that Adriano owns now...

Pietro comes into my head; he's waiting for me right at this minute. His pack of cards is always on the table when I get there. And I always go, unless I'm sick. I've never let him down before. Today is the first time. But I can't just ring. I couldn't just tell him I'm sick; I couldn't do that to Pietro. He's too honest for that.

I get tired from sitting around and because it's so dark.

I stretch out on the ground behind the boxes. I've almost forgotten that someone might come in. But I mustn't sleep, just relax a bit, can't fall asleep...

When I wake up, the ferry's throbbing! Are we moving already? It is 21:17!!! I've slept for a whole four hours!

I'm really cross that I fell asleep and that I'm hungry again. I can't feel any of the pasta from Matteo's family left in my tummy. I light up the room with my phone. There are shelves full of bags of flour, tins of fruit, sacks of potatoes, trays of eggs, cartons of milk, boxes of peppers, onions, cauliflower, jars of gherkins and beans... and I'm forbidden to touch any of it.

Nobody can stop Don Carlo

If Pietro were here he would conjure up an omelette or cauliflower baked in sauce and stuffed peppers. I go through Pietro's whole menu. I can't help it; I can never forget about real hunger.

I sneak out of my hiding place and go along the shelves, like a gangster in a chamber full of gold. A gangster would stuff all his pockets. But I only take one jar of gherkins and close the box again.

The gherkins go down the hatch like a single mouthful and I feel even hungrier than before. I can't get the beans out of my head and sneak over to them. They're in plastic packets with tasty tomato sauce. I try to think of something else. But, in the end I rip open a packet and shove a load of beans into my mouth.

I'm only on the second mouthful when the door-handle moves!! The packet of beans flies out of my hand and slithers across the floor. SOMEBODY IS LIFTING THE DOOR HANDLE!! There's no time to pick up the packet. I stumble and just about manage to get back to my place behind the orange boxes when the door opens and someone turns on the light.

I can see a man in a cook's apron through a gap between the boxes. He is older than Adriano and has a beard. I don't dare even to swallow the beans in my mouth. Perhaps he only wants to get to the sacks of potatoes, I hope. Please don't let him go to the gherkins and beans! But he goes straight to the shelf, right through the beans mess.

"Merda!" he shouts. *"MERDA!"*

He uses his apron to wipe the red sauce off his shoe and roars for Adriano. Then he runs out in a rage.

I gulp down the beans and then he's back again, with Adriano this time. What if Adriano betrays me?

"If you let something fall, then you pick it up and clean up the mess, do you understand?!"

"It wasn't me!" says Adriano.

"You're the last one who took something out of here! You're absolutely useless. Now get a cloth and clean up that mess." The man takes two tins of peaches off the shelf and goes out.

Adriano has to follow him. "I'll get you back," he hisses in my direction.

Behind the boxes I go cold all over. Our football-friendship is over. Adriano will pay me back for the beans. And he's much bigger than me!

I need to get out of the room, into the passage-way before Adriano comes back. I stumble out from behind the boxes.

Nobody can stop Don Carlo

There's only one lift and two other doors out on the corridor. One door says "Cold Room"; the other one must lead to the kitchen! Adriano is probably going to come out that door any second now. And it's too late for the lift. I press myself behind the open door. Then I hear Adriano coming out of the kitchen and into the storeroom. I hear a cloth squelching on the floor.

"Come on out!" he hisses, but I'm already as far as the kitchen door and sneak into the kitchen, through hot noodle steam, past pots and flames. There's food frying in pans everywhere and cooks shouting at each other. No one looks at me. But where should I go?!

I run to the end of the passageway; there are waiters rushing over and back loading up trays of desserts. I tag onto a waiter and just follow him. I'm almost out of the kitchen with him when I see Adriano!!! He's coming through the door at the other end and he's after me!!! I run past the waiters. "Who on earth are you?" shouts one of them. But I don't turn around and run even faster, out of the kitchen and into the restaurant. The diners stare as I duck between the tables, out into the stairway and up one level, and then another, up and up and up and then out through a door. Suddenly I'm on the top deck!

The sky is dark already. I see people standing at the railings at the back. I run in the opposite direction, along the side of the ship. But where can I go? There are lifeboats hanging above me. There's ladders leading up to them, with chains in front of them. You're not allowed to go up there. But a lifeboat is the only hiding place. I climb over the chain and up the ladder. There's a cover over the boat; I squeeze myself in under it and then slide myself to the bottom of the boat. I stretch out; I won't move another inch. I can only hear the waves and my loud breathing. And then I hear Adriano's voice.

"Where are you!" He walks past, directly under the boat. "I'm going to get you, for sure!" he shouts.

I hold my breath. Then Adriano's voice fades away as he moves further along the deck.

"Come on out!" he shouts, over and over, going on until the waves are louder than him and I can't hear him any more…

I stay in my hiding place for another half hour, not moving an inch. I hurt all over from the hard ground. I push myself up and squint out through the boat cover. There's no sign of Adriano.

Nobody can stop Don Carlo

I slide back down and turn onto my side. I can't lie on my side much longer. There's not enough space to sit up under the cover. When will we ever get to Palermo?

My tummy still feels funny. I try to get Papa's laugh back into my ear and imagine him as he opens the door. Then suddenly, I wonder if Papa will even be at home when I get there, or missing, gone somewhere or other on business. And what if he is at home but he won't come back to Bochum?! I pull the balcony photo out of my jacket and light up Biro-Papa with my phone. He's laughing. Maybe Papa is better without us? He's got sun, sand and the casino and no more Mama-rules. But I can't bear to think that. I put the photo away quickly.

The waves are still whooshing. It is still the middle of the night I haven't heard another sound from Adriano. I don't really think that he has given me away. Otherwise he would get the sack from the ship. He did hide me, after all.

My legs have gone to sleep. Otherwise I'm wide-awake. I keep looking at the clock on my phone. Half-past-twelve, quarter-to-one, almost half-past-two… at six-o-clock Mama gets back from the night shift and she always wakes me up at seven. She'll go

74

into my room and find my empty bed. And she'll see my empty money-box with the map of Italy beside it. And then she'll go straight to the telephone.

I've got to get to Papa before seven, before Mama comes into my room!

When five-o-clock comes I've had enough. It's bright already. I stick my head out again. I've been doing that all night. And now I can see land. There's a dark stripe, far away, at the end of the sea. Is that Sicily???!! It's got to be Sicily!! There are mountains!! I lean so far over that I almost fall out of the lifeboat. The waves swish by below me. The wind is blowing drops of water up at me. We're booming our way to Sicily, with thundering engines and black clouds rising from the chimney.

I squint at a white speck at the back of the thin stripe; I keep staring at it. The salty air is making my eyes burn. There's houses, there's a town! Is that Palermo??!!

And suddenly the sun is up and I can hear Papa laughing again.

The city is getting nearer all the time, until I can see apartment blocks and cranes. The houses are brighter than ours in Bochum. Palermo is the most beautiful city in the world. I can see that, even from here. It's right on the sea with mountains behind it. And the sun shines down on it every day. Bochum just can't compare!

At ten past six we boom our way into the port. The ferry hoots so loud that I'm sure it can be heard in the city. Don Carlo has arrived!! I can see people on the balconies. There are balconies everywhere! Which of them is Papa's?!

Mooring takes forever. I don't dare to move out until the ferry's snout opens and the ramps crash down onto the ground. Then I crawl out of the lifeboat, climb down the ladder onto the deck and run down the outside stairs. Even if Adriano gets in my way, he won't stop me. I'll just run past him.

When I get down to the car-deck I run past the cars and past the man in white, right out of the ferry. I jump with my two feet off the ramp and onto Sicily, the biggest football in the world! I could push everyone out of my way, even the man in white. I've done it!! Almost.

I keep going, heading towards the city, over the square in front of the ferry as far as a gate and under the barrier.

"This isn't an exit!" shouts the gatemen from his hut by the gate behind me. But I've already got as far as the car park and run between the parked cars and out onto the street.

There's a taxi just going by. I pull out my envelope with Papa's address and wave it down. He even stops because everything in Palermo is easy! Then I steam into the city in a taxi.

The balconies and street signs whizz by. I look left and right, forwards and backwards. In eight minutes time Mama will go into my room to wake me up! I've twisted my envelope to a pulp.

Via Sant'Agostino! I swing my head around. It's written on the street sign!!

"STOP!!" I shout.

Then we stop in front of number 9. I shove all the *brezel*-change into the taxi driver's hand and jump out.

The house has only one balcony that looks like Papa's. There's a chunk broken off a corner and a crack running along it, just like in my photo. The only thing missing is Papa on the balcony.

I find his name right away among all the bells; it's scribbled in biro on a little sign. Then I press his bell. Once, twice! Nothing happens.

At the fifth ring the door opens, and my arms fly out. But it's only an old woman coming out. There's nobody else. I push past her into the house and run up the stairs.

I find Papa's flat on the third floor. I can't hear any sound from inside. I'm certain Papa's asleep. You can never get him out of bed. I put my finger on the bell and keep pressing. It's three minutes to seven already. And what if Papa really isn't there?

"OPEN UP, PAPA!" I nearly hammer the door down. "OPEN UP!"

Suddenly I fall into space. The door is ripped open. I need to look a second time. Papa's standing in front of me!!! In his vest, just like me!

"CARLO?"

Papa looks the same as ever! As if he had only gone away yesterday. He's just as fat with a beard all over his face and a hairy chest. The dark rings are still there under his eyes from the night. He looks just the way he did in Bochum, when he got out of bed.

"CARLO!!" he roars now and the whole stair-well echoes.

Then I jump on him and push myself into him. It's for five months, all at once, for all the waiting at school, at meals, in bed, every day. I press my nose to Papa's chest and sniff in his cologne. I've no idea why I'm crying, I'm so happy!

Papa gives a deep laugh that shakes through me like an earthquake. And he hugs me so hard, he knocks my breath away. You couldn't pull us apart again.

I don't even hear my phone at first. The ringing doesn't get between Papa and me. I only feel the phone vibrating in my suit jacket. And suddenly I think of Mama again. She's there, worried sick, looking at my empty bed! I don't want to tear myself away. But I must, before Mama thinks that I've just vanished completely.

I pull out my phone and wipe my nose on my sleeve. Then I press the green button and hear Mama talking before I even have the phone at my ear properly.

"Carlo! Is that you?"

"Hallo Mama…"

"Where are you?! You've given me the fright of my life! I couldn't find you anywhere!"

"I'm… I'm with Papa. Everything's okay!"

"You're where? Where are you??! With Papa??!!"

"In Palermo."

"With Papa in Palermo??!!"

"I've just got here and…"

"CARLO!! That's not funny!! Where are you really? You get home here at once!! Your breakfast is on the table!"

I go hot all over. "I'm coming back! This evening, maybe. You'll have to sort it out with Papa…"

"WHAT ARE YOU TALKING ABOUT, CARLO?!" Mama's shouting now. I knew she would. "WHAT SORT OF A CRAZY IDEA IS THAT!"

"Nothing! I'm with Papa. He's just beside me. We haven't had a chance to talk about anything yet and…"

"He's beside you?! PUT HIM ON TO ME! IMMEDIATELY!!!"

I don't get any chance to explain to her that I'm only here to sort something out for us all.

Papa takes the phone. "Gabriele, why are you shouting so loud?! I can hear you all the way to Palermo" he shouts through the whole stairwell. "I'm so glad! I just fell out of the bed, straight into Carlo's arms!! Why didn't you tell me he was coming! He was just standing outside my door! You could have told me, I have a phone, after all. Or even a text?" Papa goes back inside his flat with Mama, with me behind him.

"…what scheme am I supposed to have put into his head? I had no idea! I'm telling you; he just arrived at my door!"

And then it all starts again. In German-Italian and Italian-German. I don't listen any more and I have a look around me. The flat is really just one room, with a bathroom, and there's a cooker in one corner. There's a table at one end, and a chair. The bed is a mattress. Then there's a couple of boxes. We'd get all those into the cellar in no time. Papa won't need any of that stuff in Bochum.

"Wait, I'll ask him myself!" says Papa, turning around to me. "Did you run away without a word to Mama?"

I nod.

"Yes" says Papa into the mobile. "He says: yes!" And then he starts to laugh. "Isn't he unbelievable! Just pretends he's playing football and travels all the way to Palermo!" Papa laughs louder and louder. "…I have to laugh, Gabriele! He just says… yes… of course, it's serious! But I just have to laugh…"

I spot the photo of the white-water-train hanging above the table. That used to hang over the fridge in Bochum. We're sitting in the boat, all three of us, getting soaked to the skin. I remember just how much we laughed at the photo because we all look so funny. Our eyes are as big as saucers and our mouths wide open with shouting.

"You're shouting again, Gabriele… *tutto a posto*,

Nobody can stop Don Carlo

Carlo's fine! I sort it out with him and phone you back later... no, I ring you later, *basta!*" Papa hangs up. "We'd better turn it off," he says giving me back the phone. He just pulls the cord of his landline out of the wall. Then he stands in front of me, with his two hands on my shoulders. "You're driving your Mama completely crazy! Why?!"

"I really miss you so much, honestly," I say.

"I miss you too! If you had said so, I would have jumped on a plane right away!"

"But something always gets in the way, with you..."

"What gets in the way? Nothing gets in the way! I would have got out of it, made myself free! For as long as you like!!!" Papa gives me a big kiss on the top of my head. "You're my son, Carlo! I'm so glad! You just came to Palermo! I can't believe it! You've got to tell me the whole story!! But we'll talk later. First, we need some breakfast. Otherwise I'll keel over, after all that shouting!" He goes to the fridge and opens it wide. There's only butter and two eggs inside. "I'm going to throw away that fridge tomorrow, don't need it here. You can get everything fresh, just outside the door. Let's go!"

Papa pulls on his trousers and storms out of the

flat and down the stairs with his arm around my shoulder. I go with him, like in a dream. I'm walking arm-in-arm with Papa through Palermo. We go up and down steps, through tiny lanes, left and right. Papa knows his way around. He'll sort everything out with Mama. He used to just avoid any row with Mama. "You just have to stay quiet around Mama," he used to say. "She's a bit of a pressure cooker."

As we go Papa introduces me to everyone he knows. And he knows nearly everyone. "Just look at him! This is my son! Isn't he the image of me! He's got my head, the same mouth, same eyes, hasn't he?" he keeps saying.

Then we turn around a corner and we're into the market. The market goes the whole length of the street; there's no end to it!"

"Have you ever seen such a market?" asks Papa.

I haven't. There's fruit stalls, vegetable stalls, mountains of beans. There's half a cow hanging from a hook and a real pig's head beside it! And the stall holders are roaring at the tops of their voices. It's louder than in the stadium because there's nothing better or fresher than here.

Papa stops by the fish man. Everything is so fresh here that the crabs are still crawling around on the ice.

Nobody can stop Don Carlo

"*Buon giorno*, Marcello! What do you want for a kilo of these little fellows?" Papa's pointing at the octopus.

"Nine euros," says Marcello.

"Nine euros?! I could buy myself a boat and go catch them myself for that. Nine euros! Marcello! They're only little ones. And Carlo has a belly like me, hasn't he? There's plenty of space in there to fill. Eight euros for two kilo and *basta!*"

In the end Papa gets two kilos for seven euros because he says that today is a feast day, the biggest feast ever, because I'm visiting him.

We go back home with a bag of octopus and a mountain of vegetables.

Papa chops the octopus into little pieces and throws it into the pan straightaway. I stand beside him, watching every move. I see how he fries the fish, squeezing lemon into the pan with his fist, tosses in herbs or throws a piece of octopus in the air and catches it in his open mouth.

"Hot but *buono!*" he says through the haze of oil, smacking his lips.

We eat on the balcony! It's just what I had imagined! We eat straight out of the pan in the sunshine. And the octopus smells like a hundred years of Italy because my Italian Grandma was such a good cook and her grandma too, says Papa.

At last we start on the story. Papa wants to hear everything, right from the beginning. I tuck into the food and talk at the same time. I tell him about the woman at the ticket desk and Rudi with the rags of a ticket in his mouth, about Munich and the toilet in the night train. Papa's eyes open wider and wider. Usually listening isn't really his thing but now he's listening so hard that he forgets to eat. By the time I get to the bit about the lifeboat he can't even close his mouth. At first, he doesn't believe me. I can hardly believe myself any more. But that's the way it was.

At the end Papa bangs on the table. "CARLO!! YOU ARE A RASCAL!" he roars and shoots out of his chair to reach forward and catch my face between his two hands. "YOU ARE A PROPER RASCAL!!"

I can see Papa's huge grin through his beard and I'm so overjoyed that I want to leap up and do everything that was in the postcard, all at once. I want to go into the casino, race around on the moped, roast in the sun, jump in the sea…

And that's exactly what we do.

I hold on tight to Papa from behind. The moped

rattles under us and the wind is warm on our faces. We could head back to Bochum like this! But first we head for the sea.

The beach is almost empty. We plonk ourselves down on the best bit, down near the waves. We've just pulled off our trousers when, suddenly, Papa's phone rings.

"Mama??!!" I ask.

But Papa shakes his head and answers it.

"*Ciao!*… I'm on the beach, what's up?… what are you doing… at my door?"

Papa has forgotten something, I gather, a meeting or something. Suddenly, he's under pressure, I notice. He looks at the time and can't talk himself out of whatever it is.

"*Tutto a posto*… okay, okay… I'm on my way" he says at last and hangs up. "I got to go home for a few minutes, Carlo, got something to sort out, a little business, you know," he tells me, handing me some money. "Get yourself an ice cream, okay? I'll be right back, in half an hour at the latest!"

I nod, even though I'm cross. Papa rumples my hair, then he heads back up onto the street and roars away on his moped.

I've eaten the ice cream in no time. I'm roasting in the sun, in Papa's swimming trunks. They're far too big for me but they won't fall off because I'm lying down.

Out on the sea a ferry steams away. I don't need a ferry any more.

There's a plastic bottle in front of me in the sand. I take it down to the water and fill it to the brim for Pietro. The water in the bottle doesn't look blue any more, just dirty. But I'm sure Pietro will be glad all the same.

Then I sunbathe for another while, on my tummy, on my back and then on my tummy again. I make a sand-timer with my fist and let sand trickle out. I do this, ten times, fifteen times. The half an hour is long past. I look up at the street, again and again. But I can't see Papa's moped.

I want to call Papa but my phone is back on the table at his flat. Slowly I boil up to a rage because this waiting game is back again. It feels like getting sick, getting worse by the minute.

I stump my way up and down the beach. Papa's gone well over an hour now. Nothing looks beautiful any more. The sea is grey and there's rubbish everywhere. I let my feet sink down into the mushy sand. Palermo is nothing without Papa.

Nobody can stop Don Carlo

After an hour and a half, I can't stand it any more and head towards the street. I get furiouser and furiouser as I ask directions to get to Papa's street.

As I turn into the Via Sant' Agostino I miss a breath. I spot Papa straightaway. He's at the front door arguing with a woman. What's he doing standing there, with someone else, instead of coming back to the beach?! I just don't get it any more.

"Papa!" I roar and run towards him. Papa and the woman turn around. The woman looks furious. She's ranting and raving at Papa and when I get as far as them she goes off. Papa looks as if he can't cope any more.

"WHY DIDN'T YOU COME BACK TO THE BEACH?? I WAITED ALL THIS TIME FOR YOU?" I'm really roaring at him now.

"Something turned up, you can see for yourself. I've got problems, problems, problems…" And he looks at the woman disappearing down the street.

"SOMETHING ALWAYS TURNS UP ON YOU!! GETS IN THE WAY!! I'M WAITING ON THE BEACH ALL THIS TIME AND YOU'RE UP HERE WITH SOMEONE ELSE!!" I roar. "YOU SHOULDN'T BE HANGING AROUND WITH SOMEONE ELSE!! WHO WAS

THAT ANYHOW??!"

"Doesn't matter, just another pressure cooker, *capito!* I lifted the lid and *basta!*" Papa gives his moped a kick. He really needs to let off steam. "Carlo, *Dio mio*, this world is a crazy place!"

"Because you make everyone mad at you!" I tell him.

"I!! I make everyone mad? ME! I can say what I like. It's the same all over – roaring at me! Now even you're roaring at me!"

"BECAUSE YOU'RE ALWAYS PROMISING THINGS AND THEN EVERYTHING TURNS OUT DIFFERENT!"

"What do I promise? You want to go to the beach, we go to the beach. You want to go to the casino, we go to the casino! Come on! Let's go!" he says, plonking himself on to the moped. "Let's have a nice day. Today and tomorrow, I'll sort it with Mama. Then you only have to go back the day after tomorrow…"

"I'M NOT GOING BACK," I roar, "NOT UNLESS YOU COME TOO!"

"Carlo, we're both a bit mixed up, right? Why should I come back to Bochum with you?"

"When you really want something, you will do anything for it. We'll take your stuff up out of the cellar! You can just move into my room with me."

"You're driving me crazy, Carlo. You imagine that it's all so easy, but it's complicated. I'll come and visit you, that's a promise."

"THAT DOESN'T MEAN A THING! " The words just shoot out of me. "I'VE BEEN WAITING FIVE MONTHS ALREADY!! FIVE MONTHS, TWO WEEKS AND EIGHT DAYS!!" I roar. "I'M NEVER WAITING AGAIN!!"

Papa rubs his eyes with his hands and runs them through his beard and over his mouth. But not a sound comes out of him. Then he gets off the moped, looks up at the sky and back at me, for a long, long time. He doesn't look like the sun and beach any more. I've never seen Papa look so mixed up. He fiddles with the chain on his neck and runs his other hand through his hair.

"Carlo, *Dio mio…*" he says at last and sits down on the kerb. I plonk myself beside him.

I give him a sideways look. He's completely still except for one hand twiddling the chain through his fingers. He's thinking hard; there are deep wrinkles on his forehead. We let the mopeds stink their way past us and he says nothing, for the longest time.

"Carlo…" he begins after a long, long time. "You're my son. You just turn the world upside down. You're just like me." He puts his hand on my shoulder, ever so slowly. "I don't know anything any more. But we've got to change something... make some changes, alright?"

"Yes, alright," I say.

"I just don't know how."

"You have to come back with me anyway!"

"We'll see..." says Papa.

"Nope! That's what we're going to do."

I stretch my hand out. This has got to be a deal, a proper one, like a deal between two gangster bosses.

Papa fiddles with his chain a bit more. "Maybe you're right, Carlo... you're right..." He says after a long pause. "I understand you. We'll have to give it a try... yes... I'll come with you, okay. We have to try."

At last he lets the chain go and shakes my hand, really hard. I look him straight in the eye and feel that he really does mean it.

We spend the rest of the day lying on the beach, or in the sea doing dead man's float. The sun burns hot on our bellies and I float next to Papa on the water surface. I've never felt so light.

I'm sitting at my table in the pizzeria with Pietro. I've been back in Bochum for six months. When I brought Papa home with me Mama nearly knocked me over with hugs and kisses. It was as if I had been away forever. She wasn't angry any more, just happy that I got back safe and sound. I had to spend a whole week in bed, with a fever from the night in the lifeboat and sunburn all over from the beach.

I often go off with Papa. He's back in business, in Palermo or somewhere else, but he always comes back. We've been to nearly all the home games in the stadium and even to the water park, all three of us together, with Mama. We screamed and laughed in this photo too, just like the one hanging over the table in Palermo.

The rest didn't quite come true. Papa is living with one of his thousand friends and his stuff is still down in the cellar. Mama and Papa don't get on well enough to live together, not yet anyway. That's something I still need to sort out, somehow.

I had another look at my map of Italy to see where we could go on holidays. We could all have a holiday together, that's my next plan. There's always plenty to laugh at on holidays. Then things would get better between Mama and Papa, I'm sure of it.

Pietro brings me my *Pizza al Carlo*. It's got everything you can think of on it. The pack of cards is on the table already. I look over at the bar. Pietro has put the bottle of sea water on the mirror shelf behind the bar. It's right in the middle, with plenty of space all around it. And there's a lamp hanging from the ceiling, lighting it up, like a real trophy.

"Carlo, you have to tell me again, what happened with the ticket and the dog?" he asks as he sits down opposite me.

He wants to hear it, over and over again, from start to finish. He leans back and gets his napkin ready. He wipes his bald head with it, when the story gets too exciting.

"From the start, Carlo, *Avanti, Avanti!*" he says and I start again…

Young Dedalus 2020

Nobody can stop Don Carlo
Oliver Scherz
translated by Deirdre McMahon

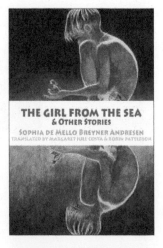

THE GIRL FROM THE SEA
& Other Stories
SOPHIA DE MELLO BREYNER ANDRESEN
TRANSLATED BY MARGARET JULL COSTA & ROBIN PATTERSON

MEMOIRS
OF A
BASQUE COW
Bernardo Atxaga
translated by Margaret Jull Costa

THE BOOKS
THAT
DEVOURED MY FATHER
AFONSO CRUZ
translated by Margaret Jull Costa